THIS BOOK BELONGS TO

_____

_____

_____

Not Yet a Yeti

An original concept by author Lou Treleaven
© Lou Treleaven
Illustrated by Tony Neal

MAVERICK ARTS PUBLISHING LTD
Studio 3A, City Business Centre, 6 Brighton Road, Horsham,
West Sussex, RH13 5BB, +44 (0)1403 256941

First Published in the UK in 2018 by **MAVERICK ARTS PUBLISHING LTD**

American edition published in 2019 by Maverick Arts Publishing, distributed in
the United States and Canada by Lerner Publishing Group Inc., 241 First
Avenue North, Minneapolis, MN 55401 USA

ISBN 978-1-84886-414-6

Maverick
publishing
www.maverickbooks.co.uk

distributed by Lerner™

NOT YET A YETI

WRITTEN BY LOU TRELEAVEN

ILLUSTRATED BY TONY NEAL

To you, whoever you decide to be.

George's grandad was a yeti.
His mom and dad were yetis.
His sister was a yeti.

My Grandad

My Mom and Dad

My Sister

All of George's family
were yetis.

All My Family

Me

All of them except George.

"When will I be a yeti?" George asked Grandad.

"When you can survive alone on a frozen mountain, waiting to lure stray hikers to their **DOOM**," Grandad growled.

"I don't want to lure stray hikers to their doom," said George.

Grandad put his massive paw on George's shoulder.
George nearly fell over.

"Then you are not yet a yeti," Grandad said.

"When will I be a yeti?"
George asked Dad.

"When you can chase people round the mountain until they **SCREAM** with **TERROR**," Dad said.

"I don't want to chase people until they scream with terror," said George.

Dad hugged him.
George couldn't breathe.
"Then you are not yet a yeti," Dad said.

"When will I be a yeti? You're one already,"
George said to his big sister.

"When you can leave a footprint in the snow that makes people **GASP** with **DREAD**," Big Sister said.

"I've only got small feet," said George. "Look."

"Then you are not yet a yeti," Big Sister said,
accidentally stomping on George's toes.

"It's not fair," George said to his mom when she came back from chasing some hikers. "I'm still not yet a yeti."

"Do you want to be a yeti?" Mom asked.

George looked inside his head for the yeti he imagined he would be. It wasn't there.

"No," said George.

Mom put on some soup. She hadn't caught any hikers that day, so it was vegetable again. "Well, what do you want to be?"

George looked back inside his head.
Finally he saw it. "I want to be...

unicorn!"

Mom stopped stirring. "Are you sure?"

"Yes!" said George.
"I'm not a yeti. I'm not even
not yet a yeti. I'm a unicorn!"

As George spoke, a sparkly horn appeared on his forehead,

his arms and legs grew hooves,

and a mane and tail swooshed onto the bits
where manes and tails go.

"Derek!" Mom yelled. "You'd better come in here! George has turned into a unicorn!"

Dad let out an earth-shaking roar.

ROAR!

George took a deep breath.

"Dad? I don't want to frighten people.
I want to help them.
I'm not yet a yeti.
And I never will be."

Dad scratched his furry head. "Well," he said,
"We do love chasing hikers.

But if we keep eating them, they'll become extinct.

So, maybe WE could chase them...

...and YOU could rescue them?"

George's grandad was a yeti.

My Grandad

My Sister

His sister was a yeti.

His mom and dad were yetis.

My Dad

My Mom

All of George's family were yetis.

All of them except George.